The Tortoise and the Hare

RETOLD AND ILLUSTRATED BY GRAHAM PERCY

For Alex

Distributed in the United States of America by
The Child's World®
1980 Lookout Drive • Mankato, MN 56003-1705
800-599-READ • www.childsworld.com

ACKNOWLEDGMENTS
The Child's World®: Mary Berendes, Publishing Director
The Design Lab: Kathleen Petelinsek, Art Direction and Design;
Anna Petelinsek, Page Production

LIBRARY OF CONGRESS CATALOGING-IN-PUBLICATION DATA
Percy, Graham.
  The tortoise and the hare / retold and illustrated by Graham Percy.
    p. cm. — (Aesop's fables)
  Summary: A proud hare brags that he is the fastest animal in the world,
and so when a tortoise challenges him to a race, the hare is confident that he
will win.
  ISBN 978-1-60253-204-5 (lib. bound : alk. paper)
  [1. Fables. 2. Folklore.] I. Aesop. II. Hare and the tortoise. English.
III. Title. IV. Series.
  PZ8.2.P435Tor 2009
  398.2—dc22
  [E]   2009001648

A slow and steady pace sometimes is best.

here once was a proud hare who loved to show off. He bragged to anyone who would listen.

"I'm the fastest animal in the whole world!" he said. "I can outrun anyone."

"And you," he sneered at a tortoise standing nearby. "You must be the slowest animal who ever lived."

The tortoise stroked his chin
and thought for a moment.
"Well, why don't we have a
race to see if you are right?"
he asked.

"Race against you?" giggled the hare. "Why, that's ridiculous! That would be no race at all!" The hare rolled around in the grass, laughing at the very thought of it.

The tortoise slowly made his way to a nearby tree stump.

"Let's start the race from here," he said. "We'll race all the way around the lake. The first one back to this stump will be the winner."

"That's easy!" laughed the hare. "I'll be back before you've even started."

The field mouse agreed to
be the judge. The hare and the
tortoise lined up. The hare was
still laughing to himself as they
got ready. The field mouse waved
a twig and shouted, "Ready . . .
set . . . go!"

The hare zipped ahead right away. He bounded and leaped on his long, strong legs.

The tortoise plodded far behind. He made his way at a slow, steady pace.

Halfway around the lake, the hare was a little out of breath. He stopped for a moment. He looked around for the tortoise, who was nowhere to be seen.

"There's plenty of time for a short rest," thought the hare. He lay down in the warm grass and was soon fast asleep.

A few hours later, the tortoise reached the hare's napping spot. He smiled to himself when he saw the hare fast asleep. The tortoise didn't stop to wake him. He kept moving along, slowly and steadily.

The hare slept all afternoon.

By the time the hare woke up, it was evening.

"Oh no!" he cried. "I overslept!" The hare ran as fast as he could toward the finish line.

Meanwhile, the tortoise was almost to the stump. Just as he stepped on the finish line, he heard the hare thundering up behind him.

But it was too late—the tortoise had won!

All the waiting animals crowded around the tortoise. They laughed and cheered for the winner. The hare couldn't believe he had lost. He was embarrassed and angry. He quickly left the celebration.

The field mouse congratulated
the tortoise.

"Well done!" he squeaked.
"A slow and steady pace is
sometimes the best!"

AESOP

Aesop was a storyteller who lived more than 2,500 years ago. He lived so long ago, there isn't much information about him. Most people believe Aesop was a slave who lived in the area around the Mediterranean Sea—probably in or near the country of Greece.

Aesop's fables are known in almost every culture in the world, in almost every language. His fables are even *part* of some languages! Some common phrases come from Aesop's fables, such as "sour grapes" and "Don't count your chickens before they're hatched."

ABOUT FABLES

Fables are one of the oldest forms of stories. They are often short and funny, and have animals as the main characters. These animals act like people. Often, fables teach the reader a lesson. This is called a *moral*. A moral might teach right from wrong, or show how to act in good, kind ways. A moral might show what happens when someone makes a poor decision. Fables teach us how to live wisely.

ABOUT THE ILLUSTRATOR

Graham Percy was a famous illustrator of more than one hundred books. He was born and raised in New Zealand. He first studied art at the Elam School of Art in New Zealand and then moved to London, England, to study at the Royal College of Art.

Mr. Percy especially loved to draw animals, many types of which can be found in his books. He illustrated books on everything from mysteries to lullabies. He was even a designer for the animated film "Hugo the Hippo." Mr. Percy lived most of his life in London.